This book belongs to

_____

This book is dedicated to all the kids who love to cook or help out in the kitchen.

Designed and illustrated by Ira Baykovska

Copyright © 2024 by Tiffany Obeng

All rights reserved. No part of this publication may be reproduced in whole or in part, or stored in a retrieval system, or transmitted in any form or by any means, electronic, mechanical, photocopying, recording or otherwise, without written permission of the publisher.

Paperback ISBN: 978-1-959075-22-6
Hardback ISBN: 978-1-959075-23-3
LCCN: 2024912392
Also available in ebook

ANDREW
LEARNS ABOUT CHEFS

part of Andrew's
"Career Day" Book Series

Tiffany Obeng
Ira Baykovska

One Tuesday in July, Andrew had been invited to a kids' cooking class and he was very excited.

Chef Amber led the class.
She would show them what to do.

She began, "Are you ready, chefs?"
And Andrew thought, *That's new*.

Then he asked, "What's a chef? What exactly do chefs do?"

Chef Amber said, "That's a great question. I'm glad you asked, Andrew!"

Chefs bring together people and food from all around the globe to share history, cultures and traditions, young and old.

Chefs create *amazing* dining experiences.
That's the ultimate goal.
To hear, "Compliments to the chef!"
is like winning an Olympic gold.

*Dawn Burrell (pictured on the left) is a U.S. Olympian and acclaimed chef.

A chef's work is fast, busy, and full of activities.
Cooking is only one of their many responsibilities.

Chefs decide what food goes on the menu and how it is prepared. And they use unique talents and skills to create recipes beyond compare.

They use science,
more specifically chemistry,
to mix together ingredients for
the perfect flavor symmetry.

And art skills to present their dishes beautifully on our plates. So we can enjoy our meal with our eyes before we even taste.

Somewhat similar to **food stylists,** have you ever heard of them?

They make food look delicious
in photo shoots and film.

But a chef's job can be dangerous
with all the kitchen hazards.
They must follow kitchen safety rules
to prevent injury and disaster.

There are different kinds of chefs, such as **head chefs** and **sous** (su).

And a number of specialty chefs
and the special things they do.

Like **pastry** (pay-stree) **chefs** make croissants, tarts, pies, and sweet treats.

Fish chefs make all fish dishes and **meat chefs** cook all meats.

Fry chefs fry everything: meats, cheeses, even veggies.

And **sauce chefs** create pasta sauces, soups, stews, and gravies.

As a chef,
you, too, can achieve great things!
Just like
Patrick Clark, **Zephyr Wright**,
Edna Lewis, and **John Hemings**.

Wow, Andrew thought
as he waited patiently
for the meal he had prepared:
a cheese pizza with pepperoni.

Andrew beamed, "Look Daddy,
I can be a chef someday indeed!"
Daddy said, **"Of course you can.
You can be anything you want to be!"**

Glossary

Dawn Burrell - represented the U.S. in long jump at the 2000 Summer Olympics and as a chef, she was a James Beard Award semifinalist.

Edna Lewis – one of the first Black women from the south to write a cookbook that did not hide her name, gender or race.

Fish Chef - makes all fish dishes, and picks which fish are in season and the best ways to prepare them.

Food Stylist - prepares and presents food for photographs, movies, television, and advertising.

Fry Chef - uses fryers to cook meats, vegetables and sometimes cheeses.

Head Chef - is the top chef in the kitchen and is directly involved in food preparation.

James Beard Award - one of the most wanted prizes honoring U.S. chefs who are creating amazing food, food media content, and more.

John Hemings - enslaved chef and first African American celebrity chef inspired ice cream, French fries, and macaroni and cheese.

Meat Chef - cooks all meats, picks the best cuts of meat and the best ways to cook meat to make it tasty.

Sous Chef - works under the Head Chef and manages other chefs of the kitchen.

Pastry Chef - makes desserts, pastries, sweet treats, and non-baked goods like custards.

Patrick Clark – first Black chef to win the James Beard Award and made French cooking popular in America.

Personal Chef - prepares meals for clients in the client's home or in the chef's own kitchen.

Sauce Chef - makes sauces for dishes including salad dressing, pasta sauce, gravy, stews, and stocks.

Zephyr Wright - personal chef to President Lyndon B. Johnson and a civil rights activist.

With your parents' permission and help, search on your computer or go to your local library or bookstore to learn more about the different types of chefs and other famous chefs like **John Young** *(the original king of buffalo wing) and* **Leah Chase** *(queen of Creole cuisine).*